KATE'S CREW

JAYNE RYLON

eBook ISBN: 978-1-941785-28-7
Print ISBN: 978-1-941785-55-3

Ebook Cover Art By Angela Waters
Print Book Cover Art By Jayne Rylon
Interior Book Design By Jayne Rylon

Sign Up For The Naughty News!
Contests, sneak peeks, appearance info, and more.
www.jaynerylon.com/newsletter

Shop
Autographed books, reading-themed apparel, notebooks, totes, and more.
www.jaynerylon.com/shop

Contact Jayne
Email: contact@jaynerylon.com
Website: www.jaynerylon.com
Facebook: Facebook.com/JayneRylon
Twitter: @JayneRylon

OTHER BOOKS BY JAYNE RYLON

<u>DIVEMASTERS</u>
Going Down
Going Deep
Going Hard

<u>MEN IN BLUE</u>
Night is Darkest
Razor's Edge
Mistress's Master
Spread Your Wings
Wounded Hearts
Bound For You

<u>POWERTOOLS</u>
Kate's Crew
Morgan's Surprise
Kayla's Gift
Devon's Pair
Nailed to the Wall
Hammer it Home

Hotrods
King Cobra
Mustang Sally
Super Nova
Rebel on the Run
Swinger Style
Barracuda's Heart
Touch of Amber
Long Time Coming

Compass Brothers
Northern Exposure
Southern Comfort
Eastern Ambitions
Western Ties

Compass Girls
Winter's Thaw
Hope Springs
Summer Fling
Falling Softly

Play Doctor
Dream Machine
Healing Touch

DEDICATION

For anyone who's been told no but trusted your gut and forged ahead anyway.

CHAPTER ONE

Kate wiped her palms on her paint-splattered cutoffs before adjusting her grip on the rebuilt window casement. A flash of tan skin drew her attention to glistening muscles. They rippled over five sexy frames as the crew renovating the townhouse next door hammered nail after nail into their first-story roof, just a few feet below her perch.

From inside the bedroom where she worked, she inched to the edge of the ladder rung then craned her neck through the opening in front of her for a glimpse of the intricate tattoo spanning Mike's broad shoulders. Instead, she caught him reaching up to their stash of supplies for another pack of shingles.

When her gaze latched onto the drop of sweat that slid along his neck, she forgot to breathe. She watched in fascination as it journeyed over his defined pecs and six-pack abs. After it was absorbed in the ultra-low-riding jeans snugged to his trim hips by a bulging tool belt, she heaved a sigh of relief.

Kate swiped at a blob of paint that had plopped onto her wrist unnoticed while she'd ogled Mike. Her tongue moistened her lips as she imagined licking a similar trail down his body. The edge of the fresh trim gouged her thigh as she strained for a better view. The gasp she made busted her. His head lifted, catching her spying. Great, now she'd never convince him to take it easy with his persistent innuendo or date invites. And, no matter how much she wanted to, she couldn't indulge either of their desires.

Mike threw her a dazzling victory grin. The anticipation sparkling in his cocky stare blasted a shockwave through her, screwing with her balance. The ladder wobbled then tipped. She probably could have righted herself if she hadn't been standing on tiptoes to maximize her view of the scenery. In slow motion, she watched his expression morph from flirtatious to horrified.

Kate flung out her arms in an attempt to catch the frame before she tumbled through it but the momentum swung her around. Her temple grazed the custom-made pewter latch she'd installed the day before. She hung, suspended in midair, as Mike rose from his crouch. The other guys began to turn toward her, but he was already sprinting for the edge.

Terror froze her insides when he launched himself across the ten-foot gap between their houses. Then she spun away, losing sight of him. She braced for imminent impact.

Shit, this is going to hurt.

Everything happened at once. Air whooshed from her lungs when she slammed, on her side, onto the roof. She rolled, flexing her ankles in an attempt to find purchase that would halt her skid toward the brink. But her knee wrenched at an awkward angle while she continued to rake over the slate. Her hand caught the ridge of an attic vent, slowing her descent, but gravity overcame the tenuous hold. Her frantic fingers recoiled from the sharp metal edge.

The gutters rushed closer, her last hope. After that, she'd have to pray the evergreen shrubs would cushion her, preventing any broken bones. The heels of her work boots hit the aluminum edging but kept going. Her legs dangled in thin air.

Then a strong hand banded around her wrist. Her arm nearly jerked from the socket as she lurched to a stop. Kate shoved on the edging shingles with her free hand, fighting to stay on the roof.

"Son of a bitch!" Mike hauled her the rest of the way up.

"Sorry, been eating too much fast food on this job." She surprised herself by squeezing false bravado past the thudding of her heart and the constriction of her throat. Mouthing off beat bursting into tears of relief in front of the construction-chief-turned-action-hero she'd lusted after for months.

"Now's not the time to be a smartass. You could have gotten yourself killed."

"It was your damn fault." She didn't wait for him before scaling the slope toward the safety of her window.

"*My* fault? We told you that ladder's a piece of shit. You're too stubborn to get a new one."

"My grandfather's ladder works just fine." She ignored his helpful boost. The way his hand spanned her ass, cupping her, would pitch her off the precipice again if she wasn't careful.

Mike climbed in so close behind her the heat of his defined chest scorched her bare arms. She attempted to leap away from the temptation of his security, but a spike of agony rolled up her ankle, buckling her knees.

His solid biceps banded around her, molding her to his chest as they sank to the floor together. "Jesus, I've never been that scared before."

No kidding.

"You shouldn't have pulled that stunt, Mike. Who do you think you are? Jackie Chan?" She struggled to break his hold before her adrenaline rush coerced her into doing something stupid, but the weak attempt didn't budge him. Unable to fight them both, she surrendered, resting her forehead on the side of his neck. She bit her cheek to keep from licking the pulse pounding within reach of her lips. "But thank you."

He framed her face, lifting it to his scrutiny. His forest green eyes widened at her automatic compliance. He stroked wisps of hair from her cheek with the knuckles of one hand. Mike's hunger etched into the rugged set of his full lips, igniting a flame of longing in her core. They leaned into each other, mouths parting, when the clomp of work boots shattered the moment.

Bulky forms honed by years of manual labor invaded all the free space in the spare bedroom. Then a chorus of testosterone-laden cheers stifled her hushed conversation with Mike.

"That was awesome!"

"Way to go, Mike! Dude, when you nailed that slide I thought for sure you were going over the edge with her." Joe leaned down to give Mike's back a solid clap. The impact jostled Kate, making her wince.

"Careful, she's hurt." James knelt beside them, running his capable hands over her arms, verifying she hadn't broken anything. She flinched from his touch but not because it hurt. Of all the guys, he seemed the most reserved— quiet, confident and sensitive. She'd been tempted to spill her guts to him on more than one of their shared breaks. But she'd never figured out how to phrase her longing without coming off like a slut. What would he have thought of her decadent curiosity?

"No, I'm fine. Really." As long as you didn't count the throbbing in her head, the zing racing up her leg every time she moved or the lust saturating her nerves at every place she made contact with Mike.

"I'm going to take her over to St. Anthony's. It looks like clear skies. We'll finish the roof tomorrow."

Though the five men were partners, Mike seemed to make the majority of the decisions. He had a knack for business, handy for managing their house-turning enterprise. They'd bought the brownstone next door not long after her grandfather had passed away, bequeathing his home to her. She couldn't count the number of times they'd sacrificed progress on their project to give her a hand with the minor renovations she'd taken on, or lent her their tools. Sometimes she suspected they hung around longer than necessary when they'd sensed her melancholy at roaming the big house alone.

She'd also lost track of how often she'd found herself daydreaming about one—or more—of them bending her over a sawhorse, their tools clanking together as they sought payback for their assistance. Or spread her out on the lush grass under the oak tree for an entirely different kind of refreshment at the end of the day.

Kate had stopped counting the depraved permutations at a million and one. But how could she watch their sexy bodies in motion, share lunch and beers after a hard day's work, or observe their camaraderie without wanting to be a part of it? Wanting them?

"Come on, Katie." Neil gave her shoulder a tiny shake that broke her from her reverie. "You're zoning on us. Let's get you checked out."

"Not necessary." She tried to smother their objections but one versus five weren't good odds.

In the end, Dave sealed her fate. "If you're not going to the doctor then you better decide who'll be camping out here tonight."

"What?" How could she choose Mike and risk leading him on or offending the others? How could she spend the night locked in here with any of them and avoid making a fool of herself?

They misjudged her alarm for outrage.

"You just took a header out the window, you're bleeding all over Mike and you're hardly able to focus. No way are we leaving you here by yourself, babe."

And no way could she control herself through a sweltering summer night with a fantasy or five hovering nearby.

"Fine. Let's get this over with. But you're only wasting your time."

They might have taken her grumbling more seriously if she hadn't blacked out the moment she struggled to her feet.

CHAPTER TWO

Sure hands travelled the length of her exposed back. A heated torso slid across her pebbled nipples. She closed her fingers around a pair of straining erections while someone smacked her ass then kissed away the sting.

Kate reveled in another steamy dream about Mike and his crew. Practice made perfect because this time she swore the heat of an intimate embrace seared her skin while she writhed on the cool sheets of her bed, half-awake. When she rolled her hips, her slick mound nudged a rock-hard shaft larger than any she'd imagined.

Her eyelids flew open to confirm her suspicions. Mike!

He was sprawled across her bed, making the queen mattress look like the rickety cot she'd slept on when camping as a kid. She remembered now. He'd escorted her home from the emergency room then refused to leave, though she'd been given the all clear.

Holy shit, she'd practically humped his leg. Attempting to hide it would be futile. His nostrils flared as he blinked against the golden glow streaming in the east-facing window.

"Morning." The sleep-roughened greeting accompanied by his sexy smile sent her heart into overdrive, but he only made it worse when he said, "Don't let me stop you. Sounded like you were having a good time."

She would have rolled away, locked herself in the bathroom for a week then ignored the whole fiasco, but he refused to let her flee. Faster than she thought possible, he flipped her to her back, pinned her wrists to the pillows with his forearms and trapped her ankles beneath his shins. The coarse hair on his legs abraded her as she struggled to escape. Every delicious rasp teased her sensitive flesh.

The weight of his cock thudded onto her belly as he closed the space between them to stare into her eyes. "Tell me now if you don't want me."

How could she lie like that? He'd be buried inside her within sixty seconds if she didn't object, but the greedy part of her screamed for her to take what they both needed now and sort out the consequences later. With a moan, she lunged up then covered his wicked mouth, devouring his stunned smile.

Mike groaned, sinking onto her. Her bruised hip protested, but she forgot all about the minor pain when he settled against her, skin on skin, from head to toe. Her instincts ran wild. She wrapped her thighs around his waist, crossing her ankles at the base of his spine.

Their tongues tangled, stroking, thrusting, licking. Her nails raked the length of his back until she grabbed his ass. The thick muscles there tensed beneath the pressure that left ten miniature crescents in the perfect globes.

When he broke the contact of their lips then rested his head on the pillow beside her for a moment, his harsh breaths buffeted the curve of her neck. "Now you...want...to rush? Damn it, Kate. I don't have any condoms."

"I'm on the pill," she whispered. "And I'm safe. Tell me you are, too?"

"I promise."

She nodded and sighed.

He dipped his head to suck on her tight nipple but she squirmed, angling her pelvis until the head of his cock bumped the mouth of her pussy. They moaned in unison. He teased her with tiny rocks of his hips that tapped the full head of his erection against her ultra-responsive tissue. After a few passes, her dripping slit transferred enough lubrication that he began sliding instead of nudging her.

The ridges of his heavily veined shaft stroked her clit while he rode the furrow of her labia. Dark hair feathered over his brow as he wandered lower, engulfing the tip of her other breast in moist suction. Her legs trembled. Each glide buffeted nerves already on edge.

Months of anticipation had made her needy. Nights of masturbation hadn't eased her desire. She didn't want to come again without him filling her.

"Fuck me, Mike." She shifted one hand to tug on the silky strands of his midnight hair, forcing him to look into her eyes. The instant he recognized the scale of her appetite, he lost all restraint.

"Shit, yes. I need you, too." He scooped his arms between her and the mattress, curving his hands so they cupped her shoulders. When his ass rose beneath her feet, gravity caused the head of his cock to sink. It dipped into her entrance.

They paused to take a synchronized breath. Then his arms flexed, the bulging sinew cushioning her as he impaled her with his erection. She screamed at the simultaneous pleasure and pain. His monstrous flesh spread her, stretching even as it fanned the raging inferno in the pit of her stomach.

He clasped her tighter, drawing her down while he thrust up until he worked his full length into her welcoming sheath. A shudder ran through her when his balls tapped her ass.

"You fit me perfectly. I knew you would." The satisfied possession gleaming in his eyes caused her pussy to clamp around his embedded hard-on. He nuzzled her neck, alternating biting with licking. When she'd adjusted to his intrusion, he began to thrust.

For the first few strokes, her swollen passage clung to his cock as though afraid he would abandon her. But his skilled mouth, roaming fingers and the circular motion of his hips teasing her clit coaxed more wetness from her until his entire girth was coated. Slick and hot he tunneled inside her, driving her to pleasurable heights she'd never before experienced.

Lasting more than a few minutes when subjected to such ecstasy would be impossible. The liquid fire spreading through her surpassed even her wildest dreams. Kate bit her lip, struggling to resist the primal urges encouraging her to crash into the best orgasm of her life. She didn't want it to be over so soon.

"Let go. I've got you."

She resisted the blanket of pleasure suffocating her.

"There's more, I promise. I'll give you more. Let go." She opened eyes. When had she scrunched them shut? Generous yet commanding, Mike left her no choice. His lips latched onto hers, drawing her tongue into his mouth, sucking in time to the rapid lunges of his hips. She had to obey.

Mike swallowed her scream when she shattered around him. She bucked, grinding her pussy into his waiting abdomen. She expected him to come with her, to end their long-awaited bout yet he preserved his restraint.

Not without effort.

She came hard, the orgasm clenching her channel. For each squeeze, she swore his jaw gave an answering clench as he gritted his teeth. He tipped his head back then groaned but held on.

His motions slowed until she wondered if she'd missed his climax. Still, the length of his shaft twitched inside her, triggering aftershocks of delight. She stroked her hand over his sculpted chest, fingers flexing in time with the periodic squeezes of her pussy.

The relief suffusing her didn't last long. In place of the mindless hunger she'd surrendered to, an undeniable yearning built within her. She had to return the pleasure this man had given her. At least this one time. Kate knew what he needed. After all, she'd refused to let him win for weeks.

With a sigh of regret, she separated their bodies. His cock abandoned her pussy with a slurp. Instead of evacuating the bed, she rolled. She presented her ass for his enjoyment as she knelt before him, shoulders flush with the mattress.

He growled. Then his hands gripped her hips as though he held on for dear life. "You trust me?"

"Of course." She trembled when she thought of all he could do to her in this position. When something nudged her rear passage, she jumped before she realized the digit was far too thin to be his cock. He swirled his thumb around the pucker before coating it with some of the juices that had spilled onto her thighs.

Kate rested her cheek on the sheet once more. She moaned when the thrill of his taboo touch sparked her lingering arousal. What would it be like to take a man there?

"Relax."

Mike teased her until her anxiety transformed into pleasure, allowing her muscles to go slack. Then his thumb sank into her virgin hole. She didn't expect it to feel so damn good. Just when she'd started to embrace the novel sensation, the bulk of his rigid cock prodded her pussy once more.

This time he glided in to the hilt. The combination of his thick shaft and his thumb in her ass had her undulating beneath him in minutes. When he leaned forward, resting his forearm across her shoulders, lightning bolts of desire struck her nervous system. Pinned under his bulk, she embraced his desires only to find she had adopted them as her own.

"Yes. Please, Mike. Take me." He answered her cry, riding her hard and fast. The knowledge that she could make him wild drove her higher. She craved the ultimate proof. The grunts he made as he slammed into her indicated she'd have her wish before long.

The thought made her muscles contract, hugging him tighter. The constriction of her pussy increased her own pleasure. She hovered on the cusp of another huge orgasm. "Mike!"

Her urgency broke through his pounding rhythm. "Yes? Tell me, Kate."

"I want you to come on me."

"Fuck!" His groin smacked the back of her thighs as his thumb rotated in her ass. Three, four more times, he pounded into her before he yanked his cock from her with a roar. The searing splash of his come on her spine triggered her own release. When her ass seized his thumb, the sensation amplified her orgasm. She came in his arms as stream after stream of his semen marked her.

She drifted in a haze of bliss with him on top of her, his heavy presence comforting. Eventually, he reached to the floor beside the bed to grab his discarded T-shirt. He wiped the evidence of their debauchery from their skin before turning her to face him. The tenderness mixed with contentment on his face spurred her to confess.

"I'm sorry, Mike. You can't stay."

He flinched, but refused to budge. When she tried to avert her face from his persuasive gaze, he captured her lip between his teeth then nipped her. "Enough. Enough running, Kate."

Her brain struggled to catch up to this alternate reality where she finally had what she wanted, but she couldn't keep it. If she could just get dressed maybe she could usher him out with a modicum of pride intact.

"What happened to our clothes?" Her question came out a bit garbled since he maintained his hold on her lip a few seconds longer. "I remember falling asleep with pajamas on."

"It's fucking hot up here at night. I'll have James take a look at the air-conditioning later. You stripped after you'd been asleep for five minutes." His eyelids drooped at the memory. "Now quit stalling. Why are you fighting what's between us?"

He dusted her mouth with his even as he left a sticky trail of arousal in the wake of his half-hard shaft, which traced a shallow arc across her abdomen. She forced her hips to stay glued to the bed instead of tipping up to align her aching pussy with the head of his cock. Even as endless passion threatened to obliterate her better judgment, guilt corrupted her bliss.

"It's not fair to do this to you," she whispered.

"To tempt me until I swear blue balls isn't some high school myth? To rile me up with those sweet smiles and naughty looks, then bolt whenever I get within arm's reach? To refuse me all damn summer until I end up fucking you like an animal before I've even taken you out to dinner? What? What exactly isn't fair about this bullshit?"

He'd never shown her even a hint of impatience before. It left her no choice but to be honest. To be direct.

"It's not fair to start something serious with you when I want to fuck your partners, too."

CHAPTER THREE

Heat crawled up her chest then progressed onto her cheeks at the admission. She'd never had these kinds of urges before. Well, maybe once or twice. But only in an abstract way. She'd never had anyone specific in mind, and she'd certainly never admitted the fantasy to a lover.

Kate had tried to discount her constant hunger for her new neighbors as a product of the steamy season, their often half-naked bodies or, even, her hormones kicking in as she got older. None of the lies held water.

Something about this man drew her like a bear to honey. And his friends sweetened the deal. Fear of his rejection had her mind racing so out of control, she didn't realize he'd started laughing until he flopped to his back on the mattress beside her.

He flung his contoured arm over his eyes, burying his once-broken nose in the crook of his elbow. The tribal armband ringing his biceps jerked as he tried to stifle his amusement but failed. Kate's face flamed even as her stomach cramped.

She slugged his shoulder. "What the hell are you laughing at? I know I'm nothing special, but I've seen the way your friends look at me when they think I can't see. Hell, I can feel their eyes undressing me every time I bend over. It's driving me insane!"

When she shifted—tucking her legs under her to scurry out of the bed—he rolled to his side, propped his scruffy jaw on his hand then grabbed her around her waist and refused to let go.

"There's no need to get your pretty panties in a bunch, doll."

"Good thing, since I'm not wearing any." She thrust her chin in the air.

"True, that." His pupils dilated. "But you're missing my point."

Mike coaxed her to recline beside him with languorous strokes of his fingers on her waist. Then he shook his head as if remembering what he'd been saying. "I can't believe you made me chase you like a rabid dog because my crew turns you on."

"It's not just that they're smoking." She cleared her throat.

"No worries. I caught you the first time around, babe. You want to get it on with them."

Kate clamped her bottom lip between her teeth then gave a reluctant nod. "I'm sorry."

"Stop it. Stop assuming you know what I want."

How had he ended up above her again? His laser stare sliced through the flimsy denials she'd hoped to construct.

"Ever hear the saying, 'Work hard, play harder'?" Mike encroached on her personal space, filling every gap with his scent, his heat and his challenge.

"What about it?" She gulped like a fish out of water.

"I've known the crew for ten years, ever since we suffered through trade school. There's not much we haven't done together. I'm a pretty open-minded guy. Would it surprise you if I said you wouldn't be the first woman we'd shared?" He traced the ridge of her collarbone with the tip of his middle finger.

She tried to answer but couldn't, her throat had gone dry.

"You think about it, Kate. Where's your feisty spirit now? Do you have the guts to go after what you want? All you have to do is ask."

Just when she thought he would steal her inhibitions with another kiss, he sprang over her then headed for the shower. On the vintage-tile threshold to the bathroom, he turned. "And, one more thing, sweetness... You're plenty special. Never doubt that."

***

Where the hell had Mike disappeared to? Kate shouldn't care, but she did. She scolded herself when she scanned the yard for the tenth time that minute. She'd spent the morning trying to ignore his insufferable smirk, as he strutted around the site, while mentally reciting all the reasons she couldn't accept his unconventional proposition.

Despite this morning's wake-up call, affairs weren't her style. The unwise urge to prevent him from walking away after one sweaty liaison had almost overwhelmed her sense of self-preservation. Instead, she'd driven her hand beneath her thigh to keep from reaching out to tug him into bed for another romp following his shower. She couldn't risk getting any more involved. No matter how she prayed she could change, she would always want more—something lasting.

The *thunk* of her forehead hitting the sheetrock patch she'd finished installing an hour ago almost drowned out her sigh. Her cell phone vibrated, alerting her to an incoming text message. Every hypersensitive nerve in her body jumped to attention.

She flipped open the phone. Mike.

Meet me in our laundry room. Come in through the garage. Quiet. Quick.

Ignoring his command would be prudent. Also impossible.

Kate sprinted along the hall then took the stairs two at a time before racing out the rear entrance. She hopped the low stone wall dividing their properties then snuck into the neighboring garage like a cat burglar working a world-class heist.

Her hand brushed the doorknob leading from the car bay into the house, where the washer and drier would one day go, but she got drawn inside before she could turn it. Mike's powerful arms surrounded her, pressing her spine to his taut abdomen. The ridge of his constant hard-on fit in the valley of her ass, covered only by the thin material of her Capri sweats and her thong.

"What—"

The astringent odor of sealant wafted up from his hand, which covered her mouth. In the pitch-black, the brush of his lips on the shell of her ear startled her. She flinched at his raspy whisper. "I want to show you something. Everyone lusts. Everyone fantasizes. When your lover respects you, you should feel free to explore your desires. No matter how extreme."

Her eyes began to adjust to the darkness. Slits of light gleamed through the louvers on the interior laundry-room door, which faced into the kitchen of Mike's fixer-upper. Now that she could hear past the galloping of her heart, she froze. A masculine moan echoed off the tiled surfaces of the vacant living space. No, make that several moans.

"Want to see what it could be like?" The plane of Mike's chest cradled her as he inched them closer to forbidden delights with shuffles of his steel-toed boots. His hands encircled her waist. The tips of his fingers teased the hem of her tank top. Then they slid beneath it to rub irresistible circles over the skin on either side of her belly button.

Kate shivered in his hold.

"Go ahead, take a peek." He bumped her with his pelvis, grinding against her.

She worried her lip between her teeth as she debated. But the next primal grunt of pleasure dissolved all traces of resistance. Before she knew what she intended, her fingers tucked in the slats at eye level and her nose smooshed against the cool, painted wood.

Oh. My. God.

From this angle, she caught the strong profiles of both James and Neil. Tall and lithe, Neil leaned on the end of the countertop for support, his jeans unbuttoned. Framed in worn denim, his cock jutted from the vee of his fly. James hovered a mere half inch away from the head. His lips parted, glistening with saliva, as though waiting for permission.

"Suck it." The gruff command reverberated through the space, causing a trickle of wetness to run onto Kate's thighs.

In the kitchen, Neil buried his fingers in James's sun-bronzed hair, using the grip to tug the kneeling man closer still. With two fingers, he aimed his erect shaft straight for James's open mouth. When he slid inside, balls-deep with a single stroke, the look of rapture on both men's faces stole her breath.

From behind her, Mike's hands travelled lower, dipping beneath the waistband of her pants. He shoved them over her hips until they pooled on the floor. "Mmm...you smell delicious. Wet already? I thought you might enjoy the show."

He cut short her whimper when he tilted her face for a scorching kiss. But he didn't steal her concentration from the other men for long. When she turned her head back, they had paused. Had they heard her?

Please, don't stop!

As though they read her thoughts, the two men resumed their rough play.

James's stout throat worked around Neil's embedded cock. She almost cried out again when his jaw slid forward, dragging his lower lip over Neil's tight sac.

"Fuck! Where did you learn that trick?" Neil panted.

"From me."

Kate's eyes widened as Dave strolled in from the living room. An impressive bulge tented the front of his cargo shorts. His hulking frame and towering stature might have been intimidating if he weren't so quick to joke or lend a helping hand when needed.

"Son of a bitch. Can't you two go five minutes without getting off?" Joe followed a step behind Dave. "We have a deadline..."

He should have saved his breath. James continued to give Neil what looked like a world-class blow job. She thought Neil's gaze flickered toward her and Mike's hiding spot, but he didn't say anything.

Joe grinned, then shrugged at Dave. "Now's as good a time as any for a break. We need them to concentrate when we snap the chalk lines for the patio or everything will be out of square, and we'll spend all afternoon fixing it anyway."

The easygoing partner stripped his shorts off in two seconds flat. His cock, bare beneath the khaki, sprang free. He put one hand on the counter then hopped up beside Neil with animal grace. When his balls rested on the cool marble they'd upgraded to, he hissed.

"Come on, Dave. I see you checking out James's ass. What are you waiting for?"

CHAPTER FOUR

James raised his hips in clear invitation. Each man embraced his sexuality without inhibitions. Every desire they expressed met with acceptance and trust from the others. The display caused a surge of hope and desperation in Kate.

What would it be like to explore her yearnings without fear of recrimination? The mere idea of such freedom had her arching into Mike's roaming caresses, craving something more.

"Shh, babe. I've got what you need." His fingertips completed their circuit around her swollen folds before retreating. The pause, filled with the faint rustle of him shedding clothes, gave her a moment to refocus on the scene before her.

Joe had braced one arm behind him. He reclined with his weight on his straight-locked elbow to give Neil the room needed to reach over and surround his hard-on with one fist. Neil had joined him on the countertop. Their thighs pressed together from hip to knee. As she watched, Neil turned his head to claim Joe's mouth in an aggressive exchange.

She'd never seen two men make out. Their whisker-stubbled jaws rasped together as their tongues clashed. They devoured each other. Meanwhile, James continued to feast on Neil's cock. His head bobbed with sure strokes on the other man's tool, eliminating the hesitancy she sometimes experienced when she wondered what her ministrations would feel like. Should she suck harder? Use more tongue?

James made short work of the fasteners on his torn jeans. Dave had positioned himself behind James, who bent at the waist between Neil's lightly furred legs. His meaty hand rubbed his crotch through his work clothes as he took in the trio of lovers before him.

The tendons in Dave's neck protruded when the golden skin of his partner's back gave way to the lighter flesh of his ass beneath his low tan line. Dave scrounged in his utility belt. When his hand landed on what he sought, he grinned.

"I was just about to start coating the bolts for the railing so they wouldn't rust." He held up a jar so Joe and Neil could see, then gave it a shake. "Let's hear it for petroleum jelly, huh, James?"

James moaned around Neil's erection then widened his stance. His steely cock bobbed between his legs. He ran his hands up Neil's thighs then cupped the other man's balls in his palms, nuzzling them with his chin. The confident massage of his stained fingers had Neil's hips bucking, driving his shaft farther into James's eager mouth.

"Put your hand on me, Neil." Joe grabbed Neil's wrist then guided it to his stiff flesh. Kate didn't blame Neil for being too distracted to function without assistance. James lapped the dripping head of Neil's cock before returning to his enthusiastic sucking.

Kate followed the line of Neil's toned arm to the juncture where it encased Joe. The flared tip beneath Neil's fingers left a trail of pre-come that glistened in the afternoon light. While Neil's lips travelled along the column of Joe's neck to tongue his pebbled nipples, Joe's gaze riveted to Dave, who swirled his index finger in the open jar.

Lost in her observations, Kate gasped when Mike's throbbing cock nudged her swollen pussy. Then she rocked against him, clamping her teeth shut over a whine when he retreated on the cusp of entering her.

"With James, babe. Imagine it's you out there, the center of all that attention."

Her pulse spiked at the thought.

Dave scooped a generous dollop of the lube onto his cock. He stroked the substantial length until it made squishy sounds against his greased palm. Then he wiped the excess jelly over the clenching pucker of James's ass.

Mike mimicked the sensation, swirling his fingertips across the mouth of her pussy, spreading her ample arousal over every exposed surface of her labia. The pleasure had turned to torture. She struggled to force him inside but he evaded her then pinched her ass.

Luckily, the men seemed oblivious to her squeak.

"No cheating." To silence her protests, he circled her mouth with two fingers until her lips parted to admit them. The sweet taste of her own arousal burst over her tongue. She realized his intent when he used the intrusion to tip her head forward, blanketing her back.

Kate sucked on his fingers as though they were Neil's long, lanky cock. She swirled her tongue over his short nails then nipped the thicker, work-roughened pads.

"Yes, that's right." He adjusted her so she could see out a lower slat. The sensual recreation in front of her blazed to life once more.

Neil and Joe stared at Dave's cock as he set the head against the tissue ringing James's asshole. Dave's hard-on, though proportional to his mammoth frame, appeared out of scale compared to James's compact build.

How will he take all that?

Dave wrapped his fingers around the base of his shaft then bounced the heavy head against James—sensitive flesh on sensitive flesh—in a series of quick slaps. The contact initiated a chain reaction. James moaned then swallowed Neil's erection, his lips circling the root. Neil cursed then squeezed Joe's cock, pumping faster.

She swore Mike trembled behind her with the effort of hovering on the brink. Almost penetrating. Yet he refused to bury his length in her.

Dave gripped one of James's hips then used his other hand to guide his hard-on through the initial resistance of his partner's ass. It seemed as though all six of them gasped in unison when the tip plunged past the broadest point to drive several inches deep.

Mike's cock burrowed inside her before she'd recovered from the delicious vision. The shock of being filled to capacity obliterated rational thought from her mind. Both her and James writhed together beneath the assault of overwhelming pleasure.

"It's been a while, my friend. Your ass is nice and tight."

"No, Dave, you're just fucking huge. Don't hurt him." Neil gritted his teeth but whether he held back pleasure—or some sort of possessiveness—at the sight, Kate couldn't tell.

A strangled groan drew her attention to Joe. "Oh, fuck. I can't watch, or I'll have to put up with you shitheads ragging on me for coming in seconds again."

The group laughed together despite the sexual tension arcing between them.

Joe bolted from his spot. He got to his feet on the countertop, straddling Neil's splayed thighs. The motion presented his crotch—at chest level—to Neil, and averted Joe's gaze from the other three guys' carnal display.

Dave chuckled as his hand snuck around James's waist to cup the man's dangling cock and balls. "Open to me. We'll go slow."

"No!" James protested around Neil's cock.

At the same time, she begged Mike. "Fuck me. Now."

Without waiting for either Dave or Mike to move, James and Kate rocked backward, taking their lovers balls-deep.

"Shit, yes!" Dave bellowed when his flat abs slapped James's ass.

On the counter, Neil surrounded Joe's cock in a double-fisted hold. He didn't offer to suck the standing man. Joe didn't push beyond Neil's limits. Instead, his hands clamped onto Neil's shoulders, braced for the ecstasy generated by the firm touch. He thrust into the grip, which hugged his shaft.

Mike spread his fingers along her pussy on either side of his cock, now shuttling in and out of her. She forgot to stay quiet when his palm rubbed circles over her clit, matching the way Dave began to jerk James in time to his steady thrusts.

The force of Mike's penetration shoved her forward. She continued to lave his fingers in her mouth while she studied James's throat working around Neil's cock. A quartet of desire filled the space with a symphony of masculine grunts and moans that sounded like music to her ears.

Kate ground her clit against Mike's other hand. The contact compounded sensations pouring through her from the thrill of witnessing such honest passion. She could've come in an instant but, somehow, it didn't feel right to climax without James and the rest of the crew. The throb in her teeth alerted her to how hard she tried to hold on—to wait for them to join her.

"Good. Girl." If his gravelly tone was any indication, Mike struggled, too.

The rapid flex of Joe's ass grabbed her attention. Despite his attempt to block out the irresistible display, he seemed like he would be the first to cave. He hammered his cock into Neil's tense grasp.

"Almost worse." Joe groaned. "Can hear you guys. Smell you. Good imagination."

Kate had to disagree there. Nothing could surpass watching this fantasy come to life.

Dave grunted as he plowed into James's ass with measured strokes that Mike imitated one for one in her pussy. "Are you gonna shoot already, Joe? You know how it turns James on to see a dude come. He'll probably squeeze my cock in half if you give him such an up-close-and-personal show."

The dirty talk nearly destroyed her resolve. The walls of her pussy began to undulate, stroking Mike's cock.

"Not. Yet." Mike tweaked her nipple with his free hand. The pain should have helped her regain control, but it shoved her closer to the brink instead.

"Shit! Yeah, I'm coming." Joe's thighs bunched as he stood rooted to the counter. His pelvis jerked repeatedly, slamming into the side of Neil's hands. His head dropped back, exposing the prominent bump of his Adam's apple, which bobbed in time to the contractions of his muscles.

Neil angled his fists toward his lower abdomen, braced when the first hot rush of Joe's semen splashed across his belly button. All of them moaned at the contrast of the white strands decorating Neil's olive skin. When Joe collapsed onto the cool counter, Neil had a direct line of sight to the pure ecstasy etched on James's face.

"Son of a bitch! You do like that, don't you?" Neil clenched his jaw.

James's cheeks hollowed as he answered with a renewed show of enthusiasm.

"Want more?"

From her vantage point, Kate knew James's response to Neil wouldn't matter. Neil had no hope of stopping himself now. Mike and Dave increased the tempo of their fucking—whether because their partners had reached the breaking point or because they couldn't help themselves, she would never know.

She welcomed the powerful lunges, watching how Dave's hips forced James's cock through the circlet of the bigger man's waiting fingers. Their tensing balls tapped together on every stroke.

James lifted his gaze to the trail of Joe's come dripping toward Neil's hard-on. He reached his tongue alongside the shaft, scooping up a hint of the viscous liquid. The hum of approval he made around Neil's cock proved to be Neil's undoing.

Neil grabbed James's hair then rode his mouth hard as Dave slammed into his ass. Neil bucked against James's lips as he released with a shout. James sucked him dry before lifting his well-used mouth from his partner's wilting cock to clean the come from Neil's abdomen with soothing strokes of his tongue.

Dave groaned as he watched James lap up Joe's semen. He rode James harder and harder until the smaller man's grip on the edge of the counter slipped. James's cheek crashed into Neil's slick abs.

Kate bit her cheek as Mike used both hands to anchor her against his violent fucking.

"Get. Ready," he uttered between clenched teeth.

"Fuck. Yes!" Dave groaned as he continued to ram inside James. "Come now. Do it."

The first jerk of James's straining cock flung a jet of cream to the floor. It also shattered her restraint. All rational thought disappeared as sensation overruled her mind. Her torso went rigid in Mike's secure grip. Her pussy milked him, begging him to join her.

By the time James had finished coming, a string of pearly fluid dangling from the tip of his spent cock, her orgasm had picked up steam once more. Mike refused to let her off so easy.

Dave pounded James. The base of his erection throbbed in time with his hoarse shouts. He filled James's ass with spurt after spurt. Mike broke the parallel, about to pull out of her pussy. She chased him with her pelvis, refusing to let him free.

"Come. Inside me." The ripples of pleasure amplified into another full-blown orgasm when he stiffened behind her then poured his seed into her welcoming grasp. He shifted his hands to her chest, cupping her breasts in his calloused palms. He continued to fuck her through his climax, setting off waves of unrelenting pleasure with the liquid fire filling her.

Either from the position, or the physical effects of her release, she grew dizzy. In the kitchen, the guys had started to clean up when Mike obscured her vision by settling her against his chest. Aftershocks continued to contract her pussy when he picked her up. She tried to focus on taking deep breaths as he dashed across the yard with her cradled in his arms, buck naked.

CHAPTER FIVE

M ike deposited her in the antique, bent-pine chair in her breakfast nook. Somehow, he'd managed to get redressed before whisking her away from detection. He reached behind his back, grabbed a handful of his black T-shirt then hauled it over his head. The supple cotton radiated his warmth when he threaded her arms through it.

The fabric that had hugged his muscular shoulders draped around her like a baggy dress. He crouched on the linoleum by her feet then patted her knee. "Fun, right?"

Fun? Blood rushed through her veins even minutes later. It throbbed in the engorged tissues of her pussy and fluttered beneath the flushed skin of her wrists.

She stammered, "That was—" *Rough. Free. Primal. Hot. Generous.* "—beautiful. But no wonder you laughed at me this morning."

"What the hell are you talking about, Kate?"

"They're gay." She wanted to sink into the earth. How conceited could she be? "I must have imagined the guys hitting on me because I was so attracted to them."

Mike's palms cupped her flaming neck. His thumbs tipped her face up with slight pressure on her jaw. "The universe has more shades than black and white. Believe me, they want you almost as much as I do. I'm no jealous prick, but I've had to watch my temper lately. You make me break all my rules, babe."

"Rules?" She couldn't imagine someone so uninhibited imposing self-restrictions.

He grimaced then shook his head. "Sorry, brain's not firing on all cylinders yet. Massive blood flow diverted."

She blinked when she confirmed the tent in his crotch. How could he be hard? She would have feared she'd never again see an orgasm the likes of the ones he'd given her if just thinking about the dirty deeds they'd exchanged in the laundry room hadn't fired her libido once more. Maybe their encounter hadn't satisfied all his needs?

"Um... Do you... Have you ever..."

He laughed, "Are you trying to ask if I'm bi, too?"

She nodded.

"I've tried just about everything once, but it's not really my thing. I'll admit, though...I've accepted more than one blow job from the crew members." He shrugged. "I'm a guy, I like getting head. For me, if it's just about having a good time, then a mouth's a mouth as long as I respect the person it's attached to."

Her knees went weak imagining his come spraying down another man's throat.

"But, I definitely like your parts best." He winked then laid his lips on hers with aching tenderness.

She bowed into his hold, soaking in every modicum of sweetness he was willing to impart. All too soon, he broke the embrace. He dusted butterfly kisses over her checks and eyelids before rising to his feet.

"Sorry to fuck and run, but we really do need to get the patio laid today if we're going to finish up by tomorrow night."

"Finish the patio?" Panic twisted her guts. Their skills had guaranteed their progress on the complete overhaul would be ten times faster than her snail's pace for even the simplest tasks, but they couldn't be done already.

"Yeah, it's the last thing on our list. The longer we hold the house, the less profit there is in turning it. So, before we start every job we set a date. If we make our deadline, we throw ourselves a wild party. Definitely keeps us motivated." He waggled his eyebrows.

It figured she'd discovered the perfect way to expand her horizons right before she lost the opportunity.

Kate pasted on a phony smile to cover the dread freezing the lingering heat from her core. If she felt anything other than disappointment over the lost opportunity, she forced herself to bury it. There would be plenty of lonely nights to examine her foolishness later.

"The pool inspector cleared our upgrades this morning so we're planning a cookout. You know, we'd love to have you as our guest of honor." He picked an imaginary piece of lint off his paint-splattered jeans.

She might have laughed if his sudden vulnerability hadn't stunned her silent.

"If you're still interested after today…"

"I'll think about it."

"That's all I can ask, babe." Mike brushed his lips over her forehead then turned away. "Stay off that ladder."

The wooden blinds tapped against the window as he shut the door tight behind him.

***

They'd slaved beneath the beam of spotlights until nearly midnight, then picked up again at the first light of dawn. Kate cursed the weather gods who hadn't answered her call for rain. Instead, the thermometer had spiked close to a hundred degrees by lunchtime. The crew dragged ass for the first time since they'd carted their equipment onto the lawn next door.

Before she could consider the consequences, she squeezed a dozen lemons into her grandmother's pitcher then grabbed a tray. As she arranged store-bought cookies on a plate, she wished she'd thought to make some from scratch.

The rays of the afternoon sun scorched her cheeks. She squinted, catching sight of James indulging in a timeout under the dense canopy of the massive oak in their yard. When he saw her coming, he patted the ground.

"As if I didn't already crave your goodies." He beamed. "Pour me some of that lemonade, and I'll be your slave for life."

She sat cross-legged beside him but didn't laugh. Somehow, their games had turned serious in the past twenty-four hours. As usual, James tuned in to her mood in a flash.

"Ah, sorry, Kate. I'd give you a hug but sweaty doesn't begin to describe me right now."

He accepted the glass she handed over then drained it in one long slug.

"What? Do I have concrete dye on me?" James scrubbed at his neck.

Thank heaven for the bright light. The heat climbing her cheeks had nothing to do with the thinning of the ozone layer. Still, she couldn't meet his curious gaze. Why hadn't she considered the guys' privacy before she spied on them?

"Oh. I see." He cleared his throat. "I didn't think you'd judge me."

When he began to rise, she grabbed his forearm. "What? James! It was the hottest thing I've ever seen. But how did you know I was there?"

"Oh shit, were you feeling guilty?" He plopped onto the lush grass with a chuckle. "For a second there you really worried me. Katiebug, you couldn't keep quiet to save your life. Plus, you forgot these..."

From one of a dozen pockets on his cargo shorts, he withdrew her favorite thong. Mike must have gone back to grab the rest of her discarded clothing.

"So you're okay..."

"Honey, knowing you were watching turned me on beyond belief. Couldn't you tell?"

"Well, you did look like you were enjoying yourself." She rested her head on his shoulder, sweaty or not.

"Sounded like you were, too." He rubbed his cheek over her hair. "So, you'll be there tonight then?"

"I...I haven't decided. Do you want me to be?"

"Hell, yes." He didn't hesitate even a fraction of a second before answering. "In my mind, sexuality is a continuum. Let's take Mike. Based on the ten years I've known him, I'd say only one out of a thousand people he finds attractive are men. And I'm not talking go-to-bed-with-them attractive but, you know, some kind of spark. For me, it's the opposite. I don't want to lose the chance to act on that rare opportunity."

It seemed so simple when he put it that way.

"I guess I just don't know how to do this. How do you know what everyone wants? Each of you must fall somewhere different. Like Neil... I could tell he wasn't into sucking Joe." Her curiosity pushed her beyond embarrassment.

"Yeah, each of us has boundaries. We respect everyone's right to do or not do as they please. No one would ever hurt you or force you to go further than you want."

Kate feared she would be the one who needed to go further than the rest. Beyond physical pleasure. At least when it came to Mike.

"But aren't there rules? Mike said something about breaking his rules?" She'd be mortified if she violated some principle out of ignorance, but Mike had dodged her follow-up questions.

"He only has one rule that I know of." James grinned. "And it's stupid. If he's in danger of breaking it, I think we're all in for a treat. He refuses to mix emotions with pleasure. Or, at least, he has in the past."

Hope blossomed in her soul, but she was scared to let it run rampant. "If he wanted me as something more than a plaything, why would he want to share me?"

"There's a difference. Do you know Neil and I consider ourselves life partners?"

"You do?" Could she really have it all?

"Yep." His grin faded as he became serious. "I'd give anything for that man. I love him unconditionally, and so I accept that he likes both men and women. He accepts that I enjoy sex with multiple partners. We never have sex without each other but, sometimes, we like to indulge in the pleasure that only comes from sharing."

They sat in silence for several minutes as he allowed her to absorb the possibilities.

"Look, Mike deserves to be as happy as I am. You two are great together. Please, Kate, I'm begging. Come tonight." James winked. "Come a lot."

CHAPTER SIX

Kate paced the squeaky hardwood planks in front of the bay window. She took another pull of the Corona with lime she'd intended to take over to the crew's barbeque. Not like those guys would drink light beer anyway.

So why am I still inside? Chicken.

As she watched, Dave and Joe roughhoused. They wrestled, attempting to dunk each other in the crystal blue waters of the refinished pool. James and Neil huddled together on the sidelines while Mike tended the grill. She reminded herself that he couldn't actually see her every time he glanced in her direction.

After today, the manscape outside her window would disappear forever.

The soft orange hues generated by the dusk blurred. She'd let herself get used to their laughter, but now they were leaving. Tonight was her last chance. If she didn't take it, they'd be gone when she woke.

Regret would destroy her.

Before she could harp on every possible disastrous repercussion—and Lord were there plenty of those—she grabbed the remainder of her six-pack, squared her shoulders then sashayed across the lawn in her best imitation of a supermodel swagger.

Five smoldering stares latched on to the bared skin between the strings and diminutive cloth panels of the itsy-bitsy bikini she'd bought this afternoon. Water drops trickled from the statuesque bodies of the men in the pool. Neil's jaw dropped open and James nodded at her. But only Mike's reaction could capture her interest for longer than a glance.

Kate inhaled then held her breath as she raised her gaze to his. How she kept from stumbling when the force of his hunger hit her dead-on was a mystery.

The silence stretched a little longer than comfort allowed so she raised the carton in her hand. "Brought some beer."

So lame.

He eyed the half-empty container and grinned. "Nervous?"

She gulped around a lie, "Not a bit."

"You're safe with us." He took the liquid courage from her then set it aside. His thick arm banded around her waist as he drew her into his sheltering embrace. The scent of charcoal and hot man made her mouth water. Puffs of air danced over her temple a moment before Mike's lips pressed against it.

Then he whispered in her ear, "All you have to do is tell me it's too much and I'll take you out of the game in a second. No questions, no hard feelings. Understand?"

Light fur brushed her cheek when she nodded against his chest.

"Good girl." He separated them just enough to catch her chin then tip it up.

His lips caressed her mouth, which curved in a smile. The prodding tip of his tongue coaxed her mouth to open. A wave of desire made her forget her worries as she got lost in sensation. "Damn, I've wanted this since the moment I met you."

His strong hands landed on her waist, lifting her until her toes dangled several inches above the new flagstone pavers. She flung her arms around his neck, matching the intensity of his kiss.

Mike carried her to the edge of the pool. As he stalked closer, the motion bumped their hips together. The solid length of his erection singed her bared abdomen through his swim trunks.

A cool breeze washed over her feet as it danced across the water below. Then slippery fingers encased her ankles, guiding her descent. Water engulfed her calves then her knees. The refreshing relief from the blistering heat of the man holding her didn't last long. Kate squirmed when Dave's teeth scraped her ass. It passed before his face as Mike lowered her into the pool. Then Dave took hold of her beneath her left arm while Joe grabbed her right.

She whimpered when Mike untangled her fingers from his nape then transferred her weight to the other men. The soft protest transformed into a squeal at the icy caress of the tiny waves on her pussy. Instinct had her draping one arm around Dave's massive shoulders and the other around Joe until she tread water between them.

Half her torso had been submerged when Neil and James joined Mike poolside. Her two supports headed into deeper water, causing her to rely entirely on them to keep her afloat. She wouldn't be able to reach the bottom here.

"Look at how hard you make them." Joe cupped her breast, the nipple peaking in seconds beneath his dripping fingers. He painted cool droplets over her satiny bathing suit until it adhered to every ridge and contour of the puckered flesh.

It became a lot easier to see what he meant as the three men shucked their trunks. Mike crouched, put one hand on the intricate tile work then leapt gracefully into the pool with minimal splash. He inched toward her, never taking his eyes from her.

James sat on the edge, dipping his feet, stroking himself as he scanned the men bracketing her. "I'm so glad you decided to join us, love."

Neil brushed James's hair away from his face. He smiled when James kissed his palm then said, "What are you waiting for? Go play. I want to watch for now."

The graceful arc of Neil's arms as he raised them above his head drew James's attention as well as hers. His muscles rippled as he leaned forward to dive into the pool. She followed his progress beneath the glassy surface as he torpedoed toward her. When he was just a few feet short, he slowed, his hair swirling around his head.

Kate didn't realize his intentions until Dave jerked the string at her hip. A moment after the panels floated away from her bare skin, Neil's lips scorched her pussy. She didn't have time to feel awkward about being touched so intimately by more than one man at once.

Dave and Joe each hooked a wrist beneath one of her knees then spread her like an offering for their submerged crew member. Neil braced one hand on each of their thighs, then buried his face in her pussy. Her eyes widened at the sensation of his hot tongue licking her followed by the cool water rushing behind his touch.

Mike's groan had her searching for him. He swam closer, taking in the decadence before him. "That's right, babe. Let them give you pleasure. It turns me on to watch you burn. They can give you so much more than I could alone. I want you to take all you can."

Neil's lips closed over her clit. He sucked with gentle pulls that had her sighing before he placed one last tender kiss over her mound and surfaced. He flung his head back, sending water arcing from his Roman features in a glistening spray. Visions of erotic mermen filled her mind. James gasped behind them, apparently as impressed by Neil's primal display as she was.

"Sweet," he panted against her lips, sharing the taste of arousal tinged with chlorine.

Mike appeared over his shoulder. Her ability to focus on anything but the raging need in his eyes dissipated. He nudged Neil to the side as he claimed her lips. She sucked on his tongue, the hammering of her pulse going double time. While he occupied her, nimble hands untied the remaining strings of her bikini, baring her.

Then he, too, sank beneath the surface to tease her swollen folds with his mouth. She tipped her head back, sparing a fleeting thought for the spectacular sunset, almost as brilliant as the way the crew made her feel. The motion exposed her neck to Dave's tongue. Neil latched onto her breasts— licking, nibbling and squishing the globes together to nuzzle between them.

Just when the swirls of Mike's mouth instigated the pre-orgasmic clenching of her pussy, he swam between her legs to surface behind her. She groaned at the loss, her head now resting on his chest. The two men holding her tipped her, raising her feet out in front of her. Mike cradled her neck and head, kissing her with leisurely swipes of his lips.

Kate's toes curled as touch after touch drove her higher. Dave and Joe slid their massive hands along her body until they supported her back and legs. She floated on the surface, her breasts heating in the humid air while the rest of her bobbed, held steady by the light grasp of her lovers.

"I need to taste more of you. I want to make you come." Neil groaned when his friends adjusted her thighs. He swam between them, inviting Dave and Joe to drape them over his shoulders. He homed in on her core. She sighed when he stopped just a fraction of an inch away from fulfilling the promise of ecstasy.

"Would you like that?" Mike's harsh breathing assured her that he would like to see it.

"Yes! Please." Her fingers dug into the thick pads of muscle covering Dave's and Joe's shoulders. The restless movements urged them to bend over her, to soothe the ache in her breasts. They complied with her wishes. Dave bit her lightly while Joe sucked her nipple tight against the roof of his mouth. The variations in their touch drove her wild.

"Relax, babe." Mike took her mouth in another scorching kiss. "We're going to give you all you can take."

Neil spread the lips of her pussy. Mike released her mouth, allowing her to watch the awe on the other man's face as he probed her saturated flesh with the tip of one blunt finger. She shook beneath the eight masculine hands stroking her. But the pleasure that raced up her spine when Neil's finger penetrated her burned brightest.

He worked her open, adding another digit to her greedy pussy. She savored the grimace of passion on his face when her muscles clamped around him. When he'd lodged his fingers in to the second knuckle, he bent to flick the tip of his tongue around her clit before kissing his way up her thigh.

She gasped then bucked so hard she nearly jerked away from his fingers. Dave's, Joe's and Mike's muscular arms banded around her, securing her in place when Neil's touch returned.

"I think she liked that, buddy." Joe's gravelly hum of appreciation ratcheted her need higher. "Do it. Make her come on your face."

This time Neil consumed her with less preparation. Neither one of them could wait for pleasantries. Mike tipped her face up. "Watch him. Look at his expression when you explode."

Three of Neil's fingers slid inside her. He pumped them with liquid glides. "You're so soft."

He groaned before transferring his mouth from the inside of her knee to her clit. He sucked the bud between his lips, sending pulses of pleasure through her body. Kate's eyelids drooped, but someone pinched her nipple. Hard.

"Keep your eyes open. Watch." Mike's command seemed impossible to obey.

Neil's rapture escalated her own. She moaned as every muscle in her body tensed, straining for release. When Neil added the slightest rasp of his teeth on her pussy she couldn't resist. She spiraled over the edge into a mind-shattering climax. He continued to eat at her until the pleasure renewed, cresting again and again.

Still, he refused to let her rest.

"You can take more, can't you, babe?" Mike pet her even as he demanded she go further.

"Yes." She would have begged him to show her how to if she could have formed the words.

"I gotta fuck her, Mike. Let me fuck her," Joe begged as he and Neil switched places.

"Do you want his cock in you?"

She nodded up at Mike, hoping he wouldn't be upset. Of course, he wasn't.

He took a deep breath then kissed her. The second their lips fused, he sank below the surface of the pool. The rush of water filling her ears sounded surreal. She should have panicked, being cut off from oxygen, but they would never let anything happen to her.

She opened her eyes. The water burned a little but couldn't overpower the renewed sense of wonder saturating her. Mike met her gaze, completely in control. He continued to kiss her, doling out his supply of air between nips of his teeth and the soothing rasp of his tongue.

After several long seconds, he squeezed her hand then rose. A tiny prickle of unease sent even more adrenaline pumping through her system but—before she could freak—he returned, kissing another breath into her lungs. They fell into a rhythm of fulfillment that left her head spinning.

Just when she grew accustomed to remaining submerged, a few inches below the surface, the men lowered her another foot or so. Dave's and Neil's cocks bobbed against her hips. She surrounded the stiff flesh with her fists, loving the way they jerked in her grasp. Before she could gloat, Joe appeared between her spread legs. His hard-on looked huge through the distortion of the water.

Mike fetched another breath of air just as Joe set his erection against her still-throbbing flesh. She moaned, surrendering the last of her reserved oxygen. The instant the bubble broke on the surface, Mike returned. He claimed her mouth as Joe buried himself insidae her then began fucking her in short, fast strokes that had her poised on the edge of another orgasm in minutes.

Kate squeezed her fists around Dave and Neil. She tried to stroke their cocks but sensory overload left her uncoordinated. Instead, they began to thrust between her fingers in time with Joe. His cock shuttled in and out of her pussy. She arched her spine, trying to rub her clit against his pelvis but the harder she pushed, the farther away he got.

Dave's hand plunged into the water, landing low on her belly. His fingertip teased her clit as Joe began to fuck her faster. Mike braced her shoulders against the motion, keeping her still to accept his partner's pounding thrusts even as he continued to feed her oxygen at regular intervals.

When Dave's finger circled her engorged flesh, she knew she couldn't last long. If the quickening pace of Joe's thrusts were any indication, she realized she wasn't alone. When Mike returned, she bit his lip, trying to tell him how close she was.

He smiled and nodded before rising once more. Then Dave's finger tapped her clit in an irresistible pattern. She exploded around Joe's pistoning erection. Contractions milked his cock. She couldn't tear her gaze away as he whipped out of her. His shaft flexed. Spurts of fluid jetted from the tip to float in the liquid before her.

As though she'd triggered a chain reaction, Dave's cock bulged in her grip. Then he too sent ribbons of pearly come spiraling into the whorls and eddies made by their writhing bodies. She trailed her fingertips down the two cocks in her grip—one spent, one not—to fondle their balls.

The men raised her to the surface. Their harsh breathing, groans and awed compliments were distant in her ears. She curled into Mike's outstretched arms, seeking refuge for a moment, trying to catch her breath.

"Don't tell me you've had enough already?" he teased against her soaked hair.

Kate's Crew

CHAPTER SEVEN

Though she could hardly believe it, her body roared to life at the promise of having Mike—the man she craved—inside her. James stood at the edge of the pool, watching as their lovers abandoned the depths for dry land.

"That was the hottest thing I've ever seen." His dilated pupils and throbbing cock reminded her of the way she'd felt the day before, watching him take the three men with them now. He crouched down then extended his arms to her. She wrapped hers around his deceptively strong shoulders, clinging as he stood, lifting her from the pool.

Torrents of water sheeted off her, drenching James, but he didn't seem to notice.

Mike levered himself up, following two steps behind as James carried her toward a cluster of deck chairs near the grill. Mike lowered the seat until it became horizontal then lay out on his back. "Yo, Neil, toss me the lube."

When he snatched the tube of gel arcing toward him, she shivered in James's arms.

"It's okay, love. You'll see. It's not so difficult to take him in your ass. He'll make sure you enjoy it."

James's calm reassurance helped her battle the nerves trying to protest louder than the adventurous side of her spirit. After all, she'd already had two amazing orgasms. She turned to him, hesitating, to gauge his reaction a moment before her lips met his. The way he touched her melted her heart. Gentle. Sweet. Still hungry.

"Stay with me?" she begged against his lips. "Help me."

"Of course." James lowered her into Mike's waiting arms.

Mike cradled her back and shoulders against his torso. His cock, already greased, slid across her damp skin at the base of her spine. He leaned forward to nip her earlobe then his arms bracketed her ribs as he cupped her breasts from behind. "Are you sure you're ready for this?"

Kate glanced up into James's steady eyes. He nodded.

"Yes. Please, take me."

Mike groaned. He slipped his finger between her cheeks, teasing her as he had the morning before. This time she barely flinched when he pressed inside her tense hole.

James knelt on the chair between their spread legs. He covered her face in dozens of light kisses that had her relaxing into his touch. Mike's finger sank deeper as her muscles loosened.

Kate licked a line across the seam of James's lips when he paused to look into her eyes. He took the invitation to capture her mouth, this time with more force.

At some point during the kiss that reheated her blood to boiling, Mike had added a second digit to her ass. The forbidden touch sent a shaft of pleasure ricocheting around her body.

"Keep breathing, love." James drew her attention back to him.

She matched his measured inhalations and exhalations as he coached her through extracting every ounce of delicious sensation from Mike's ministrations.

"Son of a bitch, that's sexy," Dave praised them from the place he'd taken at her side. She realized that Neil and Joe had joined them as well. They stood in a semi-circle around the head of the chair, watching as Mike and James prepared her.

"I need you inside me." She wriggled her ass, trying to align with the head of Mike's cock. His erection felt so hot and hard against her lower back, she couldn't believe he hadn't exploded yet.

"Not like that." James nipped her lip. "Let Mike lead."

She went completely slack in their hold.

Mike moaned as the other men cursed or sighed at her submission. He tucked his cock against her ass then began to burrow inside.

Kate shrieked as the intrusion sent a lick of fire up her spine. She tensed, her pleasure receding.

"Relax, love." James resumed his passionate kisses as Neil took her hand in his, petting her until the first wave of pain passed. The tiny circles Mike made with his pelvis began to flood her with pleasure, obscuring her discomfort.

Mike pushed in farther, stretching her bit by bit, until—somehow—he'd filled her. Once inside, he raised her until just the head of his cock remained buried then lowered her until she sheathed him completely.

"Fuck, yes," he growled in her ear. She angled her head to kiss him, snuggling into his chest now that no space remained between them. His hands cupped her hips, lifting and dropping her as he continued to rock. How did he keep showing her new things, taking her higher than she imagined?

Any lingering unease flew from her mind when his long fingers cupped her pussy, then spread her labia. Bare, open to the men's perusal beneath the now-dark sky, she shivered though she didn't think she'd ever be cold again.

"So pretty."

She'd almost forgotten James, who knelt between her legs, staring at her pussy.

"Can you take us both, love?" The muscle in his jaw jumped as he waited for her to respond.

Kate held out her arms, welcoming him into her embrace.

"It's been a long time since I've made love to a woman. I don't want to hurt you. You seem so delicate." He circled the purple head of his cock around her opening, collecting her wetness. His hard-on brushed Mike's where it lodged inside her.

"You couldn't hurt me. Please, James." She gathered him close, tilting her hips as far as she could with Mike buried to the hilt. When James pressed into the slick heat of her pussy, they both groaned.

"So tight, love. So hot." He began to move, tucking into her farther with each twitch of his hips.

Kate couldn't believe how packed she felt. Her pussy practically strangled his cock. The way her two lover's erections caressed each other through the thin membrane separating them fueled her desire. Soon she bucked between them, loving the way one would retreat as the other tunneled deeper.

When he had stuffed her pussy with the length of his throbbing cock, James rested his forehead on her collarbone. She stroked her fingers through his hair then down his back. Her nails dug into his ass, trying to force him closer.

"Oh, shit. Do that again, Katie." Neil's harsh rasp reminded her they had an audience. "Spread his cheeks for me."

She did as he commanded. When James's cock flexed, triggering a massive constriction of her muscles, he and Mike groaned together.

"That's right. That's the way." Neil appeared over James's shoulder. "How would you like to try fucking and being fucked?"

James's cock flared inside her. When he turned his head to engage Neil's mouth, Kate's head dropped onto Mike's shoulder. She could only go along for the ride. She knew the instant Neil had penetrated James's asshole. The man between her thighs cried out then shuddered with pure pleasure. Neil began to drive inside James, causing the cock buried in her pussy to grind into her.

Mike stayed still, allowing the motion of their lovers to sway her on his erection. The subtle fucking stroked hypersensitive nerves, providing more than enough friction to elicit a response from them both.

"Babe, I think Dave has a present for you." Mike's suggestive tone had her gaze flicking to the side. Though he'd come in the pool, Dave's hard-on oozed pre-come from the flared head.

She gladly accepted his offering, her lips surrounding the thick shaft, reveling in the taste of his pleasure. Knowing the sight of the four lovers turned Dave on spurred her to take as much of him as she could. Pinned in place, she accepted his assistance when he cradled her head in his huge hands and fucked her mouth with gentle strokes.

"Joe, why don't you feed James some of that meat. Don't let it go to waste." Something about the position seemed so right, harmonious. Mirror images, perfectly balanced. Mike fucked her ass while she lay on his chest. James fucked her pussy while Neil fucked his ass. She sucked Dave from his position on one side of the chair, and James did the same for Joe on the other.

Ragged breathing, grunts and the squeaking of the poor abused deck chair filled the night air. Surrounded by pure desire and honest ecstasy, none of them had a chance of lasting very long. Neil drove them all higher by riding James faster, harder.

When James's tight abs stroked her clit, she tensed.

"Oh, yeah. Kate's going to come." Mike's reverent whisper cut through the group. Each man picked up the tempo, shoving her beyond restraint.

She shattered around Mike and James. After a moment, they both followed, filling her with pulses of their come. Neil shouted at the same time Dave shot into her mouth. She swallowed reflexively until he slipped from between her lips. She continued to explode, her orgasm endless.

James groaned when Neil deserted his clenching hole. "She's still coming. Yes. Yes!" James's cock flexed in time with her contractions.

Her mouth latched onto his when his orgasm crested again. A second, weaker round of come spurted from his cock, searing the lining of her pussy.

After a minute, he bussed her forehead. Then he, too, withdrew.

"Thank you, love."

When Mike pulled out, Kate pivoted. She wanted to kiss him but was afraid of his reaction when another man's seed glistened on her lips. She shouldn't have worried. He cupped her neck then drew her head to his for a searing kiss. She shared the taste of Dave's come, of all the ecstasy that had filled her, then drooped against his heaving chest.

She felt his chuckle when one of the guys said, "I'm hungry but I think you charred the burgers, dude."

***

Kate bolted upright in bed. Disoriented, she checked the clock on her nightstand. Two a.m. The delicious soreness in her joints at least relieved her that she hadn't been dreaming about Mike's crew again. She'd really done it.

She'd taken them all and loved every second of it.

So why did she feel like crying? Why did she feel more alone than ever?

"Everything okay?" The tender question from her right terrified her. If she looked, and he was just a figment of her imagination, she didn't think she could survive. "Babe, are you all right?"

Mike.

She sobbed in relief. To hell with hiding her feelings any longer. He'd shown her the beauty of trusting your lover enough to bare your soul. Your desires. And what she desired most was lying in bed with her right now.

"Oh God. Were we too rough? Where does it hurt?" Mike knelt beside her, cupping her cheeks in his palms.

She shoved his hands away, not wanting to give in to the temptation they would surely bring once he realized she hadn't been injured.

"It will only hurt if you leave me," she whispered, surprised at the scratchy tone of her voice, hoarse from her earlier screams.

"Leave you? Kate, why the hell would I leave you?" He flipped on the bedside lamp, then returned to peer into her eyes. "You don't get it, do you? All the time we've spent together this summer—laughing, working and wanting each other—only dug me deeper. I wasn't asking you out just to sleep with you. I'm not going anywhere...unless you make me."

"Never." Her heart raced ten times faster than it had by the pool. She wanted to give him the world. "So, what's *your* wildest fantasy?"

"I'd..." He cut off then blew a breath toward the ceiling, unable to finish.

"What could you possibly be afraid to say after what we just did?" She trailed her fingertips along his cheek.

Mike's sheepish grin sent shivers along her spine. "I'd like to make love, sweet and slow. Then build something lasting. In this house...with you."

"That's a dream I share. Make it come true. For us both."

He lowered her to the bed then covered her eyelids with tender kisses. She welcomed him home with open arms.

WHAT HAPPENS TO JOE AND
THE REST OF THE CREW? KEEP
READING TO FIND OUT!

For a tasty birthday treat, add four men and stir.

Note to self: When confessing a crush on an ultra-hot construction worker to your best friend, make sure he's not standing right behind you.

If Morgan thought spilling the beans on her lust for Joe would scare him off, she couldn't have been more wrong. Following her birthday wish gone awry, the hunk is treating her to one surprise after another. From little things that make her smile to lavish, romantic dates, Joe is turning out to be the stuff of dreams

Joe's attentions to the sexy pastry shop owner begin as lighthearted fun. Until he finds out about the past that, until now, has made her keep him at arm's length. Determined to show her seeking pleasure is no crime, he sets out to fulfill her steamiest fantasies—with a little help from three of his best friends.

After a four-course birthday adventure, which presents Morgan as the sweetest imaginable dessert, she expects Joe to walk away. But now that Joe's brought Morgan out of her shell, he's hungry for something he never expected to crave—a forever kind of love.

EXCERPT FROM MORGAN'S SURPRISE, POWERTOOLS BOOK 2

organ aimed a puff of breath at the flame dancing on top of the candle.

"Wait! Too fast! Didn't you make a wish first?" Kate jerked the plate holding Morgan's cupcake out of the trajectory of the warm air. The orange glow dimmed but didn't extinguish. "There must be something you want."

Carnal visions burned hotter than the fire melting the sprinkle-coated frosting of her gourmet confection into a golden pool. The color reminded Morgan of the burnished skin of her crush. It should be illegal for Joe to gallivant without a shirt on as often as he did. Spectacular memories of his displays sparked her fantasies at the most inopportune moments of the day and wreaked havoc on her sleep patterns.

Kate was polite enough not to hound her while she let her gaze wander, devouring the glistening expanse of Joe's perfect shoulders. Morgan sighed when she thought about the painted wooden sign he'd crafted—and now hung— outside the plate-glass window of her fledgling bakery. It bore the name he'd helped her brainstorm. Sweet Treats.

So thoughtful. And sexy as hell.

It kind of surprised her not to see steam rolling off his bunched muscles. How could he be comfortable working half-naked in the brisk autumn air? She shook her head. The motion didn't erase all the naughty ideas sabotaging her rationality. The dirty thoughts tempted her with a variety of ways to warm the handyman up when he finished his task and rejoined them inside.

Morgan sighed when a snap of fingers returned her attention to the interior of her admittedly cute shop. It'd taken six months to decorate everything just so.

"You going to pick something… maybe someone? Or are you planning to wait until wax drips all over your birthday cupcake?" Kate chuckled.

Morgan decided denying her infatuation with Joe would be futile. Kate had been her best friend since grade school. The lucky bitch had referred the hunky craftsman and his crew of skilled friends in the peak of the summer heat— after she'd scored the crew's foreman for herself.

No way could Kate miss Morgan's similar craving.

The crew had taken on odd jobs, fixing up the crummy space in the strip mall that housed Morgan's boutique in exchange for loads of the decadent goodies she whipped up. Damn, those guys could eat. She wondered if manual labor accounted for all of the voracious appetite they possessed. It had to take more than swinging a hammer to burn off those calories. Lord knew they found some way to stay fit and trim.

She'd baked Joe's favorite today—a caramel apple tart. He deserved that and more for his considerate gesture. Two customers had already stopped in to say the colorful sign had caught their eye. Thanks to him, she'd sold out of brownies and cheesecake long before the after-work rush. Too bad she couldn't generate the nerve to offer him something a little more sinful than her luscious dessert as a reward.

She'd considered it once or twice before, but she couldn't stop drooling long enough to try. Always quick to flash his toned abs and rock solid biceps, Joe kept her off balance and lost in a haze of unvented desire. He'd become her favorite treat weeks ago. An instant addiction. Thoughts of him left her craving a taste—or more—of him in the dead of night.

She bit her lip when he reached for something along the roofline. From his perch on the ladder, his body rippled with strength.

"Damn, Kate. I don't think the birthday fairy would sanction what I have in mind." Morgan grimaced at the dopey grin on her friend's face. Three months of blissful dating and wild nights with her boyfriend, Mike, had turned the woman into a ridiculous ball of giggles with a perma-smile. Worse were the googly eyes that emerged when the love of her life entered the room. Kate and Mike's soul-deep bond was hell to be around.

Jealousy didn't exactly flatter a girl.

"The big 3-0's not until the weekend anyway." Morgan pried her stare from Joe.

"I know but Mike and I will be out of town then, so it counts today. Besides, you'll never know if you don't try." Kate squeezed Morgan's hand. "Sometimes dreams come true. Believe me."

Yep. There went that grin again. "Your face is going to stick like that if you're not careful."

Kate kept right on beaming.

Morgan swallowed hard then scrunched her eyes closed. She was tired of hoping Joe would ask her out. So she tried a new tactic instead.

I wish I had the courage to ask him on a date. It's time to move on. Time to try again. I wish I could take a risk—be wild for once in my life.

When she blinked into the amber autumn light streaming through the window, Joe had vanished. A cosmic sign? Or had he needed some extra tool off his pickup?

"So… Was Joe the only guy involved in that wish or did some of the other hot construction workers we know feature in it too?"

Morgan's mouth gaped open. More than Joe?

She never would have confessed to greed that titanic on her own, but Kate knew her better than anyone. Morgan had thought about it. A lot. The way the guys worked seamlessly together on projects made their bond impossible to ignore. When they'd crowded upstairs—in her tiny apartment over the bakery—for beer and cookies, they'd overflowed the cramped space with testosterone and something a bit more elusive.

Their camaraderie transcended their partnership. At least she thought it did. But she could have imagined the inside jokes, meaningful looks and secret smiles more common between lovers than friends.

The men's intimacy could have been a figment of her overactive imagination but there was no mistaking their open arms. They'd accepted her right away, making her more than just a friend of a friend. Every time Morgan witnessed the interplay between the partners, her mind had spun with possibilities. That didn't mean she had to say so. "Isn't it one of the cardinal rules of wishing—if you tell, it won't come true?"

"Come on, you don't believe that nonsense do you?" Kate joked but persisted with a wiggle of her brows. "Fess up. You've wondered what it would be like to have them in your bed. At the very minimum, you're burning up the sheets with Joe in your dreams."

"Okay, fine. How could any woman resist? They're buff, hardworking, playful, sexy as sin and sweet. I've got it bad for Joe. So damn bad. Like, worse than our Bon Jovi lust in high school bad. He's strong but gentle. I could talk to him for days. He's always surprising me with little things that make my day. And the way he fills out those ripped jeans has me thinking I'm going into cardiac arrest every time he bends over. But the rest of the crew isn't far behind. Hell I'm so distracted, I've burnt more cookies since they've come around than in all the rest of my life."

"About time you admitted it."

Morgan's heart froze at the deep rumble over her shoulder. It kicked in triple time when a broad hand settled on the side of her neck. She jerked from the retro-dinette chair she and Joe had salvaged and restored last weekend.

The sneaky bastard caught the vinyl-covered seat, saving it from crashing to the floor. Would he do the same for her if her jellied knees gave out?

"You set me up." She gaped at Kate, betrayal and humiliation burning her cheeks.

"No, I'm sorry." Her best friend stood, reaching out, but Morgan scooted further into the corner to avoid her seeking grasp. "I didn't know he was there. I swear."

"I came through the kitchen. Left my boots out back so I wouldn't track mud all over the place." Joe waved toward his socks. His grin turned feral. "But I won't pretend to be sorry about what I heard. You want me. Bad."

"Jerk!"

"Maybe. But only because I've let this shit go on too long." He scrubbed his hands over his eyes. "You're so skittish. I planned to take things slow. I thought if I didn't pressure you, you'd get comfortable with me. With the guys. I didn't want to chance things. Didn't want you to run."

"Tell him why, Morgan." Kate's soft advice rankled. "Tell him about—"

"Hell, no. Not now. Not after this." Morgan's hands flailed in the air. Her glare whipped between her best friend and the stud she'd made a fool of herself over.

"Kate, maybe it'd be best if you did a little sharing of your own."

Joe had never used that stern tone in Morgan's presence before. She hated how it dampened her panties when she wanted nothing more than to escape. It wasn't as if she could take back her declaration. Upstairs, she could lick her wounds. Maybe in a year or five she could show her face around her friends again.

"I…" The other woman attempted to speak but had to clear her throat and start over. Twice.

Her hesitation glued Morgan's sneakers to the floor.

"You have nothing to be ashamed of, Kate. Neither of you do." Joe stroked her friend's hair.

Morgan had to swallow the acrid burn of envy.

Kate nodded. "When Mike and I first started dating, I told him about a fantasy of mine. I wondered what it would be like to have more than one man as a lover. At the same time. The crew granted my wish. They shared themselves with me. And Mike."

Holy crap. Had Morgan heard that right? "You mean..."

"Yeah, cupcake. The six of us had a smoking affair. One hell of a pool party." Joe's gorgeous green eyes went glassy as he remembered. "I'm not going to lie, the crew has messed around before. With other ladies...and sometimes by ourselves."

The proud set of his jaw, as if he prepared for a blow, ticked her off. Couldn't he tell how much the revelation turned her on? She'd swear her nipples were about to poke through her shirt, and her thighs trembled. This time the reaction had nothing to do with fear.

"You expect me to run screaming? Rant at you?" How many women had rejected him after finding out about his sexual proclivities?

"Maybe." He shrugged then leaned against the counter, his shoulders relaxing.

"It's not something you learn about your friends every day." Kate winced when Morgan turned her attention toward her.

"How can you think I'd judge you? You've always been there for me." Morgan tilted her head as she studied her friend. "If anything, I'm upgrading your status from lucky bitch to queen of all lucky bitches. Damn you for not spilling the details right away. What's the use in having a best friend if she doesn't come running to gloat about five of the sexiest men on the planet ravishing her?"

Kate beamed as she lunged across the gap between them and threw her arms around Morgan.

"But...one question." She sensed both Joe and Kate holding their breath as she tried to rein in her disappointment enough to keep it from coloring her tone. "Why twist my arm about how much I want Joe—"

A growl startled her into meeting his forest green eyes.

"—if you already have dibs? Shit, I didn't mean to step on any toes." Her stomach lurched at the thought of damaging her dearest friendship.

"I think you should field this one." Kate held her palms out toward Joe.

He paused for several seconds before speaking. "It's not like that between us. I mean, we all knew Mike was serious about Kate. Never seen him mope around like a lost puppy before. I laughed when she had him chasing his tail for months. Maybe that's why I'm gettin' some of my own damn medicine lately."

Kate giggled. "Mike's enjoyed the payback for sure."

"When things started heating up between them, he came to the crew. Told us about her request. I can't explain what it's like with the guys. I'm not great with words. But I can say we're closer than brothers. Comfortable with each other—with what each of us needs and what our limits are. That doesn't mean we're in some kind of relationship though. Except for James and Neil. They are pretty much a pair for life. Man, this is clear as mud, I'm sure."

Morgan didn't realize she'd moved until her fingers rested on his tensed forearm. Explaining didn't come easy. The corner of his mouth tipped up at the contact.

"I guess the bottom line is we respect each other. Kate's one of us now. It doesn't mean anything beyond that, though. We're all adults. I may not be the sharpest tool in the shed, but I see her and Mike are in this for the long haul. If they want to share some of their joy with the rest of us then we'd be glad to join in. If not, we get that too."

"The guys in the crew see other people all the time." Kate shot her a poignant stare.

It was now or never. Morgan drew a deep breath then prayed birthday magic could work in her favor. Just this once. "So... If I asked you to check out the autumn festival with me tomorrow night—"

"I'd do this." Joe wrapped her in the heat of his muscles and squeezed her tight. He dropped a kiss on the tip of her nose before teasing the seam of her lips. She parted for him, but he didn't delve inside. Not now. Not with Kate staring at them, her hands clasped in front of her, standing on tiptoes, her eyes wide.

But the lingering tingle Joe's lips had inspired promised much, much more to come.

Morgan groaned then licked the spot he'd singed with his caress. Mmm... "You've been stealing cookies off the cooling racks again."

Somehow the Belgian chocolate she'd used in them tasted better after mixing with Joe.

"I'll make it up to you." The power of his grin caused her stomach to do flip-flops. "Tomorrow night. I'll pick you up at the bakery's booth around seven."

"Who'll take care of—?"

"Let me worry about the details. You like my surprises, remember? I guarantee you'll have a good time."

Morgan tried to convince herself she'd be satisfied with some mulled cider and a run through the infamous corn maze with this gorgeous man by her side. But when he patted her ass on the way out, she swore she wouldn't settle for less than a very naughty hayride.

***

You kids have a good time. And don't do anything we wouldn't do." Mike and Kate shooed them from the bakery stand with a wink and a nod.

"I understand if you don't want to leave." Joe turned to Morgan after measuring the line of customers. It stretched out the entrance of the old barn that housed vendors at the annual festival. He didn't blame the hungry crowd. The assortment of sweet creations looked almost as tasty as his date. Almost.

"No. Let's get out of here while we can. The store will sell out soon. The last of the stock I brought is on display now."

"Congratulations. I knew it wouldn't be long before the rest of the town caught on."

"Thanks." Her megawatt smile flanked by killer dimples stole his breath. The rare glimpse made him feel like a photographer on safari who captured never-before-seen wildlife behavior. Maybe now that things were looking up with her business, Morgan could learn to smile more. "Besides, Kate owes me for yesterday."

"I'm pretty sure I owe her."

Morgan cleared her throat and adjusted the hem of her light brown sweater over the seam of her faded jeans. He wondered if the fuzzy fabric was as ultra-soft as it looked. With any luck, he'd find out for himself before the night ended.

A rambunctious toddler veered into their path when she escaped from her harried mother. Joe cupped his hand around Morgan's elbow and steered her out of the chaos. Yep. The sweater caressed his palm, tempting him to burrow beneath it to the warm flesh inside.

Damn, he was screwed. He'd planned to take things slow, but weeks of keeping his distance threatened his restraint. He forced his grip to relax, afraid of spooking her again.

"Everything okay?" Morgan's cherry-scented breath tickled the side of his neck as she leaned closer to speak over the din of the throng and the music belting out of the local radio station's amplifiers.

"Uh…yeah." He stifled a groan. "Hoping you like what I have planned."

"Planned?" She tilted her head then peeked up at him from beneath the long, dark lashes that emphasized her gorgeous, dove-grey eyes. "I thought we were going to hang out at the festival?"

"Something like that." Joe grinned at the anticipation in her glance. He loved delighting her with little things and hoped she'd react as well to what he had in store for their evening. The way she lit up shifted something in his gut. And made him wonder about the man she'd nearly married last year. What kind of damage had that asshole inflicted?

Kate had refused to give him details no matter how hard he'd pressed, but it was clear the prick had hurt Morgan. Deeply. He intended to try his best to erase the sadness he'd sensed lingering inside her—hoped she'd let him be more than a rebound guy. But he'd settle for healing if he had to. If he could. It infuriated him to see such an amazing woman hiding from the world and herself.

One step at a time, buddy.

"How about we start with a hay ride?"

***

Oh crap! Morgan blushed at the suggestion. Had Joe plucked the dirty thought from her mind yesterday? If she were so transparent, why would he pursue her instead of shoving her away like Craig had when he'd finally realized all she desired?

"Are you allergic to hay or something?"

She hadn't realized she'd stopped dead in her tracks until the pressure of his warm fingers singed the back of her arm.

"Uh, no. Sorry." Morgan studied the tiny scuff on the toe of her black leather boots. She hadn't worn them in quite a while, but the extra height afforded by the stiletto heels eliminated some of the disparity between her and Joe. In the commotion of preparation for the festival, she hadn't had time to search for polish.

"Why do I make you so uncomfortable?" His tense tone drew her gaze to his handsome, if rugged, face. The corners of his plump lips pinched together as though he hadn't meant to speak aloud. "I would never do anything you don't want. But, if you're more comfortable staying around here that's fine too."

Morgan couldn't stop herself from turning into the solid bulk of his chest and giving him a quick, one-armed hug. "Thanks for offering, but that's not necessary. I trust you."

Crazy but true.

She'd spent most of the summer with this man, alone as they worked on her store or surrounded by his equally burly friends. Funny how they'd never once intimidated her in the cramped space. Around them, she felt safe.

His smile answered for him as he dropped a kiss on her forehead. They resumed their leisurely pace toward the edge of the gravel lot where several tractors towing platforms, ringed with hay, waited for a full load of passengers. His knuckles stroked the sensitive space between her fingers as he held them in a loose grip.

A mix of children hopped up on candy, parents enjoying the brisk but not too chilly evening and young couples out for an evening of local entertainment piled into the wagon. Joe paused to boost a straggling kid onto the loose bales before leaping up himself. He turned and offered his hand. She gladly accepted. He tugged her into his arms as a few women nudged over to make room for his wide shoulders. When it looked like they'd run out of space, Morgan peeked toward the next wagon.

Instead of making a move in that direction, Joe settled in the gap remaining then scooped her into his lap before she could object. Not that she would have. The leather of his jacket smelled divine and quickly warmed with the heat of her cheek, pressed to the supple material. The woman to their right shot Morgan an envious grin before resuming her conversation with her friends.

The cramped space forced Morgan's hands to land against the taut muscles of Joe's chest beneath his thin T-shirt. Defined lines tempted her to trace them downward to the ridges of his abdomen, but she resisted. Barely.

"Comfortable?" He nuzzled her temple while his hands ran along the length of her spine. One settled on her knee, and the other on her waist, for several seconds before she remembered to respond with words instead of a simple purr.

"Very." Holy shit. Had that husky sigh come from her? Thank God for their chaperones or she might have been tempted to throw decorum out the window and beg Joe to touch her more intimately right here and now.

"Blanket?"

Morgan blinked up at the attendant waving a quilt in their direction.

"Sure." Joe winked when her mouth gaped into a giant O. "Wouldn't want you to catch a chill."

Between the helpful older man and her date, they bundled her under the well-worn cover in a matter of moments—right along with Joe's wandering fingers. She laughed when he traced the dip of her side beneath the hem of her sweater. Amid the banter of the other passengers, no one seemed to notice.

Her brows rose when Joe's palm cupped her ribcage, the side of his hand brushing the underside of her breast. No way could his touch be accidental. The warm hold soothed her. She relaxed further into the cushion of his thighs, chest and arms.

Joe flashed a terrible imitation of an innocent grin then proceeded to ask her questions about the new assortment she'd planned in order to capitalize on the change of seasons. They talked about the successes and failures of her recent product testing as the tractor began to pull them along the bumpy farm grounds toward the pumpkin patch.

To avoid embarrassing herself, she thought of things she had to do this week. That way she might be able to ignore the contact of their bodies shifting against each other and the hard length of Joe's denim-clad erection at her hip.

Before she left tonight, she'd snag a basketful of local produce to use in the tarts she'd unveil this week. "Do you like pumpkins? I have some new recipes I'd like to try if you don't mind being my guinea pig."

Her question came out more like a squeak.

"I'll eat anything of yours. After tonight, I have a feeling pumpkins may be my new favorite vegetable."

The children at the front of the wagon sang off-key loud enough she couldn't swear she'd heard him right.

Before she could clarify, the cart lurched to a halt.

"I think this is our stop."

"Huh?"

"We're getting out. Come on, you'll see." Joe set her on her feet as the attendant collected their cover.

"Don't forget, the last ride comes by at midnight. After that you're on your own to make it back to your cars. If they haven't turned into pumpkins by then." The man laughed at his own joke.

Joe planted one hand on the rail then leapt to the ground with a hell of a lot more grace than she could muster. He wrapped his hands around her waist then lifted her from the wagon as though she weighed about as much as a bag of confectioner's sugar.

Her body slid along every hard inch of his on the way down.

Oh my.

The man in the wagon tossed Joe a flashlight then trundled off into the dark toward the main barns they'd started at. In the wake of the raucous gathering and the sputtering diesel engine, the still night rang in her ears. Vines curled across the ground, their leaves rustling in the soft breeze.

They stood in the middle of the farm's pumpkin patch listening to each other breathe for several heartbeats.

"Okay?" Joe spoke softly but his gentle question might as well have been gunfire. It sliced through the quiet. "Your phone works out here if you want to call the cops on me for abducting you or have Mike kick my ass."

"Not necessary." She shivered a little, but it had nothing to do with fear and everything to do with the excitement of being truly alone with the man she'd been dreaming of for weeks. Her curiosity grew by the second. "What are we doing out here?"

"Right this way, you'll see." Again he took her hand, entwining their fingers. Suddenly it was enough to be here, with him, walking side by side along a slightly wider row in the field.

A beam of light swept from edge to edge, guiding Morgan out of danger of twisting an ankle in her ridiculous boots as long as she kept to her toes. The heels made her calves look fantastic, but had no place in the tilled dirt.

The row narrowed, forcing her behind Joe. She hummed when he tucked her fingers into the waistband of his jeans. So warm. But even that distance made the walk treacherous in the moonlight.

Rocks and divots in the earth waited to trip her. She stumbled a bit before her eyes adjusted after the bright white of the flashlight. Joe stopped in front of her. She plastered herself along his backside before she could reverse her momentum. Pure male strength greeted every inch of her from the hard tips of her breasts to the soft curve of her belly, which met his firm ass.

Morgan took a step away, thanking all the powers of the universe he couldn't spot her face flaming in the shadows or smell the scent of her instant arousal.

Instead of continuing on, Joe crouched, holding his arms out from his sides.

"Hop on. It's not far from here but I don't want to spoil the fun before it's begun."

When she simply stood and gawked, he glanced over his shoulder.

"What, you don't like the idea of riding me?"

Jesus. It was either admit she enjoyed the thought all too much or pretend her panties hadn't drenched at their collision and his naughty implication. Without another objection, she climbed onboard.

The powerful shift of his torso between her thighs had her groaning before she could prevent the sound from escaping. His fingers stroked the back of her knees. The motion, designed to soothe, instigated a hormonal riot of massive proportions.

"Too fast?" Joe slowed to a pace that jostled her less but caressed her core with each tread of his long stride.

She didn't attempt to answer. Clinging tighter to his sculpted chest, laying her head on his solid shoulder and surrendering to her hunger before it raged out of control seemed wiser. Her lips brushed his neck with each step, but sensory overload prevented her from fidgeting. If she moved her head, her rock-hard nipples would stroke his shoulder blades. If she adjusted her hips, her steaming pussy would graze his lower back.

Why was that a bad idea again?

Her tongue nipped out to taste Joe's nape. Salty spice and oak. He cleared his throat. Could she make it hard for him to speak too?

God she hoped so.

"We're here." He released her thighs slow enough she had time to ensure her footing despite her wobbly legs. She relinquished her hold on him one finger at a time. Too bad their destination hadn't been another five miles, or five hundred, away.

Joe turned to face her, blocking the view behind him. He took her hands in his, his thumbs brushing the sensitive centers of her palms. Then he lifted them over her eyes. "Don't peek. Give me a minute, okay?"

"Would now be a good time to tell you the dark isn't my favorite thing?"

"I'll be right here." The deep timbre of his voice continued to croon to her as he moved to the left then the right, a little further away then close again, so she never felt alone.

A whoosh carried to her ears a moment before heat and orange light washed over her cheeks.

"Can I look now?"

"Sure." His breath teased her face as he took his place behind her, wrapping an arm around her waist and drawing her back against his chest.

Morgan peeked between her fingers. "Holy crap!"

The digits slammed closed once more. That couldn't have been what it looked like. She must be dreaming again. But when she opened her eyes, his surprise hadn't vanished. Her jaw hung open far enough to swallow a handful of bugs. Fortunately, the brisk air kept them away.

"Is that a good holy crap or a bad holy crap?"

She couldn't answer immediately. A knot as big as a squash grew in her throat as she scanned the small pavilion sheltering them from the chill. A fire pit blazed in the center of the space, perfuming the air with the scent of applewood from the neighboring orchard.

Carved pumpkin lanterns of every size and shape ringed the perimeter of the cement-slab floor, hung from wires over the rafters and perched on sporadic wooden pillars. A few more made an elaborate centerpiece for the picnic table, laden with Indian corn, gourds, cider and other autumn treats. Geometric shapes glowed and bobbed with the radiance of the tea lights within. Warmth and welcome washed the entire space.

"You did all this for me?" She studied one of the beautiful designs so he couldn't see the sheen of moisture in her eyes.

"I did it for us," he whispered into her ear a moment before he cupped her chin in his fingers then angled her jaw until she couldn't avoid the sincerity in his gaze. "I wanted our first time together to be special. As special for you as I know it will be for me."

ALSO BE SURE TO CHECK OUT DIVEMASTERS!

COMPLETE SERIES – 3 BOOKS IN 1

Three SCUBA instructors, who happen to be sexual dominants, are about to take the ultimate plunge. If you're extraordinarily lucky, you'll be invited to join them on The Divemaster, where work and pleasure go hand in hand. Welcome aboard!

GOING DOWN

Archer Banks relishes his carefree lifestyle. Together with friends and fellow divemasters Miguel Torrez and Tosin Ellis, he travels the world, SCUBA diving by day, entertaining lonely female tourists by night. Until his father dies, instantly transforming Archer from a beach bum to a billionaire by shackling him with an enormous, undesired inheritance.

With the help of his family's longtime butler, Archer is determined to turn his new golden handcuffs into a golden opportunity. He prays Miguel and Tosin will come along for the ride when he repurposes his family's mega-yacht into a vessel well-suited for both work and hardcore play.

Never in his worst nightmares does he expect their maiden voyage to be such rough sailing. Not only is Archer's old crush, Waverly Adams, among their passengers, but the men have also stumbled upon a vast sunken treasure—one worth killing for.

Waverly surprises Archer with an alluring naughtiness he never got the chance to experience in their younger days. Busy accepting the challenge she issues his dominant side in The Divemaster's onboard club every night, he might be distracted and short on sleep. But could he also be blind to more dangerous facets of her personality?

When the divemasters can no longer deny there's foul play at hand, will Archer be going down with the ship, cursed by his family's fortune, or will Waverly turn out to be the woman of his most wicked dreams?

GOING DEEP

When her mentor is killed in a lab fire, all his notes destroyed with him, marine biologist Sabine Reynolds is determined to finish his work—a cure for an aggressive form of cancer. She needs a specific coral to continue. To find it, she boards The Divemaster to search the waters around Hawaii.

Crewmember Miguel Torres helps facilitate the collection...and brings out a sensual side of Sabine she hadn't known existed. In the warm tropical waters, she discovers fascinating things about herself and the taboo fantasies she'd never experienced before meeting the sexy guide, who isn't afraid to take charge during their daytime, and nighttime, adventures.

The Divemaster crew come face-to-face with danger in the form of rival researchers, who'll stop at nothing to ensure their success at Sabine's expense. Sabotage, theft, kidnapping, murder, whatever it takes to produce—and profit from—the cure first.

Can Miguel keep Sabine safe and by his side? Or will her enemies put a stop to her research...permanently?

GOING HARD

As the last lone wolf of The Divemaster, Tosin Ellis doesn't plan on partnering up anytime soon. Then his friend Archer commissions an engagement ring for his fiancée...

Jeweler Kahori Akama is sensual, intriguing, and happy to accept Tosin's help sourcing the black pearls she uses in her popular pieces. As their relationship goes from professional to personal, Tosin also learns Kahori's family is being threatened by someone intent on ruining her business to lay claim to its valuable property.

Tosin never expected to find a single woman that could slake his sexual appetites, but Kahori surrenders to her raw and primal urges with the natural power of a typhoon strong enough to blow even a veteran sailor far off course. Once he's experienced loving in the eye of the storm, he can't imagine being satisfied by less.

Once more, the crew of The Divemaster will do what it takes to protect their own. Especially Tosin, who realizes Kahori's heart just may be his home.

EXCERPT FROM GOING DOWN, DIVEMASTERS BOOK 1

Archer Banks's ringing cell trampled the tropical night symphony composed of lulling waves, chirping bugs, and rustling palms. He would have fumbled around on the nightstand to silence the racket if an armful of bronzed, slender woman hadn't stopped him. After rolling the beach bunny off his chest, he settled her gently on the edge of his double bed. Refusing to be distracted by her wild, sun-bleached mane, or the way the moonlight streaming in the window highlighted her damn-near-perfect ass, he forced his dick's attention from the adorable snuffle she surrendered as she burrowed into his lumpy pillow.

Archer turned his back on all that natural beauty. He rebelled against everything in his soul by lunging instead for one of the only remnants of offensive technology he allowed to intrude in his life. He didn't have a choice, really, since the hunk of plastic threatened the integrity of his eardrums by refusing to shut the fuck up.

Only one contact in the entire world had been programmed with the specific God-awful racket that now blared from his phone. The man who was instructed to interrupt Archer's solitude only in a life-or-death emergency.

Fuck. Fuck. Fuck.

Phone in hand, halfway unlocked, he launched himself from the freshly laundered sheets, which smelled of sunshine and ocean spray. He growled to the caller, "Don't expect me to rush to that bastard's side for some kind of deathbed confessional."

Archer figured he maybe should have said hello first. His bitterness had rushed out like pus from a festering wound before he could manage anything else. Odd, since he would have sworn these old injuries were scarred over by now.

"No need. He's gone." The familiar voice on the other end of the line, thousands of miles away, made Archer more homesick than the news of his own loss. "It was fast. Painless. Though probably traumatizing for the young ladies your father was attempting to have sex with when the stroke hit."

"Jesus." Archer stumbled across the room. He slipped out the sliding glass door that led to a half-rotten deck barely big enough for a pair of plastic chairs, then down the three steps to the beach. Naked, he sank onto his knees in the sand. He glanced over his shoulder toward the woman whose name wasn't nearly as memorable as the way she'd sucked him off before getting him hard again, then riding him with thighs powerful enough to cling to a breaching humpback.

Brittany! That was it. He was *almost* sure.

Was he turning into everything he'd spent his entire adult life trying to distance himself from? Had his father remembered the names associated with the assassin pussies that had finally managed to take the bastard out?

Archer's stomach churned at the thought. Acid seared his esophagus. Just like it had before he'd left that world he'd never belonged in. He hadn't looked back since. Not even for a glimpse of the girl he'd abandoned, who wouldn't welcome his attention after what had happened.

This was definitely going to be the second worst night of Archer's life.

"Sir?"

He shook his head when the question came softly—kindly, even—from his family's butler, who'd been more like a true relative than any Archer shared filthy blue blood with. It was the reason he'd borrowed the guy's name when he'd fled and remade himself. "Come on, Banks. You changed my shitty diapers plenty of times. Don't you think formality is uncalled for? I've never been that person. Much to my father's disappointment—"

"Archer." A soft chuckle warmed Banks's tone this time. "That might have been true once. But not always. Over time, I think he might have envied your escape. Admired it, though he was too proud to admit such things. Or maybe he respected you too much to go against your wishes and contact you to let you know."

"I highly doubt that." Archer swallowed hard against the feelings he'd thought he'd buried deeper than a pirate's treasure. He might be a thirty-one-year-old man, but some small part of him would always regret that he hadn't been able to be the son his father wanted.

"Well, this is for certain. He didn't truly disown you. You were never cut out of his will. In fact, despite your wishes, he left you everything."

"Shit! *Everything*?"

"His entire holdings. All of it, down to the last cent." Banks delivered the most devastating news of the night.

Everything Archer had never wanted had finally caught up with him. Golden chains ensnared his wrists and ankles, keeping him from imagining he could ever move freely again. He'd seen firsthand what it took to run an empire.

As quickly as a barracuda snaps up its unsuspecting dinner, Archer had gone from beach bum to billionaire.

Fuck him, life as he knew it—and *loved* it—was over.

He scrubbed his hands through his hair and caught sight of the woman he'd left in his bed dressing hurriedly by the light of the wall-mounted gooseneck lamp before blowing him a kiss and heading for the door.

At least he'd gone out with one hell of a bang.

Literally.

"It's not exactly a death sentence, sir."

"Banks," he growled.

"I mean...*Archie.*"

The shock of hearing that long-lost nickname, right now, had Archer blinking fiercely. Somehow he didn't think there was enough salt in the air to blame his reaction on that. "It feels like it. I'm proud of who I am these days. I don't want the money. I don't want to be like him. I can't afford to lose myself."

He scrunched his eyes closed. It was as if he were a recovering alcoholic who'd been offered an entire chain of distilleries. Archer knew unimaginable wealth could corrupt him. It hadn't been easy to sacrifice everything once, but he'd quit superfluous material possessions cold turkey and had never been happier than he was here, with next to nothing.

Good friends, a job he loved, willing women, and time to enjoy life. Those things were priceless.

"So we'll give it away. Form an umbrella foundation that supports any number of charities, funds, and projects for worthwhile causes. A lot of problems can be solved with seven billion dollars, give or take." Banks's solution seemed genius. Simple yet complicated at the same time.

"Perfect. Will you help me? And by help me, I mean run it. Make the day-to-day decisions. I don't need to know the details. Use your judgment."

"Of course. If that's still what you want, after you've really thought about it some," Banks promised. "I am the estate's executor. It will take some time to settle things. Let me see to the legalities, and you start dreaming about who you'd like to help. This fortune could change the world."

"I...uh... Okay, thanks." Archer couldn't believe this was happening. "Name it after yourself. Call it the Banks Foundation."

He had to make sure his father's name wasn't included. No glory for that fucker.

"I suppose that's naming it after *us*, isn't it?" Banks sounded pleased with that. At least he didn't mind that Archer had appropriated his name in his attempt to go incognito.

"Make sure you pay yourself, too. A shit-ton. Ten times whatever you think is an outrageous salary. You deserve a hazard bonus for the decades you've put up with my family's shit. God knows I couldn't do it. As if that wasn't obvious when I bailed."

"I will." Banks laughed, then said warmly, "For the record, I'm proud of you, too. Dream big, Archie."

ABOUT THE AUTHOR

Jayne Rylon is a *New York Times* and *USA Today* bestselling author. She received the 2011 RomanticTimes Reviewers' Choice Award for Best Indie Erotic Romance.

Her stories used to begin as daydreams in seemingly endless business meetings, but now she is a full-time author, who employs the skills she learned from her straight-laced corporate existence in the business of writing. She lives in Ohio with two cats and her husband, the infamous Mr. Rylon.

When she can escape her purple office, Jayne loves to travel the world, SCUBA dive, take pictures, avoid speeding tickets in her beloved Sky and—of course—read.

Made in the USA
Las Vegas, NV
26 November 2024

12693299R00087